*con•spir•a•cy [kuhn-SPEER-uh-see]:

a devious plan formulated in secret
by two or more persons

To Suzi & DJ — CS
For my sneaky sweet Yolanda — CD

Text © 2015 Carrie Snyder
Illustrations © 2015 Claudia Dávila

Owlkids Books acknowledges the financial support of the Canada Council for the Arts, the Ontario Arts Council, the Government of Canada through the Canada Book Fund (CBF) and the Government of Ontario through the Ontario Media Development Corporation's Book Initiative for our publishing activities.

Published in Canada by
Owlkids Books Inc.
10 Lower Spadina Avenue
Toronto, ON M5V 2Z2

Published in the United States by
Owlkids Books Inc.
1700 Fourth Street
Berkeley, CA 94710

Library and Archives Canada Cataloguing in Publication

Snyder, Carrie, author
    The candy conspiracy : a tale of sweet victory / written by Carrie Snyder ; illustrated by Claudia Dávila.

ISBN 978-1-77147-050-6 (bound)

    I. Dávila, Claudia, illustrator II. Title.

PS8587.N785C35 2015   jC813'.6   C2014-905505-6

Library of Congress Control Number: 2014947495

Edited by: Jennifer Stokes
Initial art concepts by: Marion Arbona
Designed by: Claudia Dávila

Manufactured in Shenzhen, Guangdong, China, in October 2014, by WKT Co. Ltd.
Job #14B1127

A   B   C   D   E   F

Publisher of Chirp, chickaDEE and OWL
www.owlkidsbooks.com

THE CANDY CONSPIRACY

A Tale of Sweet Victory

WRITTEN BY

CARRIE SNYDER

ILLUSTRATED BY

CLAUDIA DÁVILA

OWLKIDS BOOKS

WARNING:
Do not ~~eat~~ read this
book if you are hungry.

Welcome
to
CANDYVILLE
MINE. NO EATING!

Have you heard of Candyville? Where lollipop trees grow beside rivers of root beer? And paths are paved with peppermints? And powdered sugar falls like snow? And children eat as much candy as they want? *Mmmmmmm.*

But it wasn't always this way.

Once upon a time, Candyville was ruled by a Juicy Jelly Worm.
The Juicy Jelly Worm had a Juicy Jelly Tail, and a Juicy Jelly Giggle,
and a Juicy Jelly Belly.

Every day in Candyville, the Juicy Jelly Worm slurped up the whipped-cream throne. Gulped down the jujube crown. And crunched Cupcake Castle. (Can you say "Cupcake Castle" five times fast?)

Every day, the children whipped up a new throne. And jujubed a new crown. And fixed the castle with frosting and freshly picked cupcakes.

But the children never got to eat a bite. Ever. If a child so much as nibbled a nougat, the Juicy Jelly Worm threw a Juicy Jelly Fit.

TIP: Only Juicy Jelly Worms and Very Cute Toddlers can get candy by throwing fits.

Don't try this at the grocery store.

The Juicy Jelly Worm was selfish. That luscious field of licorice? "Mine!" Those scrumptious gum-drop trees? "Mine!" That field of candy corn? "Mine! Mine! Mine!"

The children were tired. They were hungry. They were mad. (Well, wouldn't you be, too?)

Some children plotted to steal candy. Others plotted to lock up the Juicy Jelly Worm.

"But wait!" said a clever child. (Maybe that child was you.) "I have a better idea."

KEEP OUT!

TOP
SECRET!

KIDS ONLY!

Hidden behind a tall wall of sunflowers,
the children dug a secret garden. The children
planted special seeds. The children waited.
And, my, how their garden grew.

One fine day, the sun rose like it always did over Candyville. It seemed like an ordinary morning…but was it?

"Crunch" went the castle, "slurp" went the throne, "gulp" went the crown.

"More!" cried the Juicy Jelly Worm. "More, more, more!"

Here came the children with buckets of frosting. Skipping children. Giggling children. Children with a plan.

"Mine," sang the Juicy Jelly Worm. "Mine, all mine—"

"Ahem," said the clever child.

WARNING:
Turnips ahead!

"Keep Out?" read the Juicy Jelly Worm. "Top Secret!?"
"Kids only," said one child. "No Juicy Jelly Worms allowed."
"Never mind," said another. "You wouldn't like it anyway."
"You can't stop me!" roared the Juicy Jelly Worm, barging through the sunflowers.

Suddenly, the Juicy Jelly Worm stopped and gazed in wonder upon an enormous field of…

"Candy?" gasped the Juicy Jelly Worm. "Beautiful candy? Rows and rows of CANDY?!" The Juicy Jelly Worm jiggled with excitement. "Mine! Mine! Mine!"

WARNING: That's not candy! Shield your eyes.

cherry tomatoes

peppermint

sugar snap peas

"Sugar snap peas? Yum, sugary, yum!
"Candy cane beets? Yum, sticky, yum!
"Sweet potatoes! Peppermint!
Cherry tomatoes! Huckleberries!
Purple potatoes! Turnips!"
    (Turnips?)
"Butternut squash! Sweet red peppers!
"Best candy ever!"

sweet bell peppers

sweet potatoes

WARNING:
Children have died from eating their veggies. Tell your dad.

The clever child stepped forward. "Do you like our garden?"
"I love your garden," said the Juicy Jelly Worm. "I will eat it up!
Mine, mine, mine!"

"Stop! Drop the net!"

Poor Juicy Jelly Worm. So snorty. So sniffly. So hungry for candy. (*Shhhh*—veggies!)

The clever child patted the Juicy Jelly Worm. (Was that child really you?) "I have an idea…"

"Oh, tell me, tell me!" The Juicy Jelly Worm wiped away great big Juicy Jelly Tears.

The clever child took a bite of a watermelon radish,
chewed, and smiled. "I was thinking...how about a trade?
Your kingdom for our garden."

"Deal!" said the Juicy Jelly Worm.

"For real?" The clever child spat out the watermelon
radish. (It tasted nothing like watermelon bubble gum.)

The Juicy Jelly Worm was too busy jitterbugging
to notice. "Mine, all mine! Mine, all mine!"

TIP:
Worms, like parents, are
easily fooled. Scientific fact.

"Sweet feast!" cried the children. "Sugar fiesta! Popsicle party!"
"Carrot carnival!" cried the Juicy Jelly Worm. "Lettuce leaf lollapalooza!"
"Candied apples on a stick!" they all cried together.
And everyone lived juicily jellily everly afterly.

WARNING:
This story has no moral.

Let's pretend it's about sharing.
Parents like stories about sharing.